For Jackie, Kathy, Ann, and Jeff—friends whose innate gift
of making others shine always leaves me twinkling.
—L. B.

For anyone who has had to suffer hearing me sing.
—M. H.

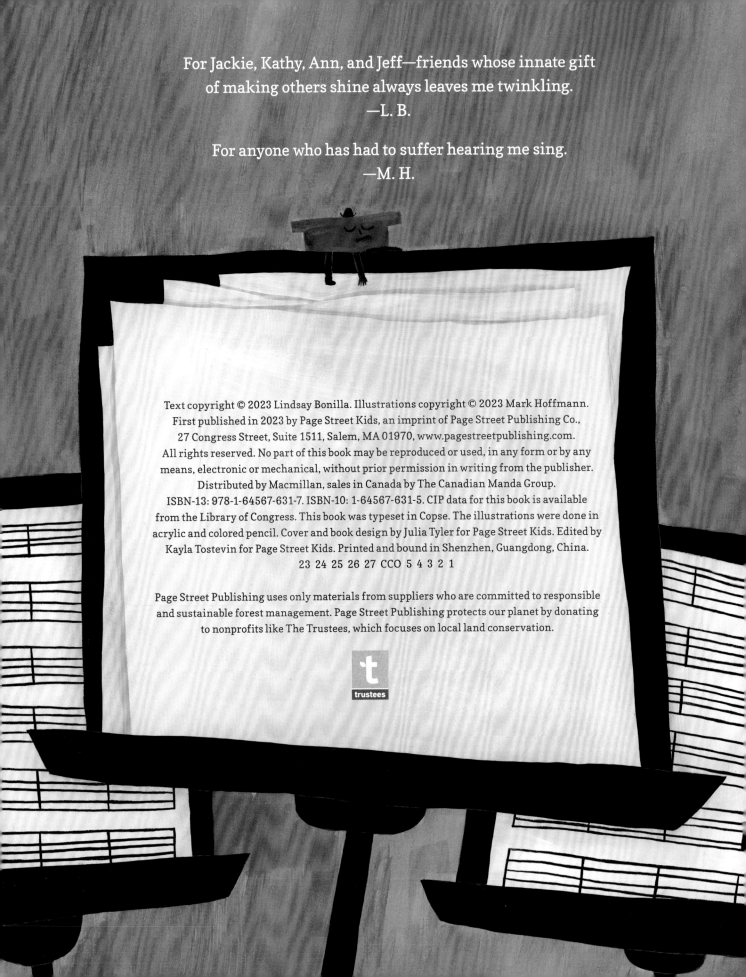

THE NOTE WHO FACED THE MUSIC

LINDSAY BONILLA

illustrated by MARK HOFFMANN

 PAGE STREET KIDS

Half Note didn't feel whole.
She watched from the side of the staff as Quarter Note and
Eighth Note jumped and jived to a toe-tapping tempo.

"Music to my ears!" applauded Composer.

But Half Note pouted. "Why do they get to have all the fun?"

"We'll be in the next piece," said Whole Note.
"I'm sure of it."

Half Note sighed. "I hate having two beats.
Why can't I be more like you? You're so confident!
And you can fill a whole measure!"

Whole Note swelled proudly.
"I can't help that I'm so big and
BEA-U-TI-FUL.
Not everyone can have four
whole beats like me."

"You're not helping, Whole Note!" scolded Quarter Note, still
bouncing as he returned from the rollicking riff. "Composer says
we're *all* important to the musical staff. If it makes you feel any
better, Half Note, I'm only one beat—half your size."

"I'm even smaller than that," chimed in Eighth Note.

Half Note's stem flopped.
"But you're so quick and upbeat! *And* you get a cute little flag!"

"Oh, give it a rest," said Whole Rest. "You'll feel better after a nice long snooze. I always do."

Within seconds, Whole Rest and the others were snoring.

But Half Note couldn't sleep.

"It's time to face the music. I'll never measure up.
The staff will be better off without me.

"Goodbye," she whispered to her friends.

The next morning, Composer sat down at his desk.

His head was full of mesmerizing melodies, riveting
rhythms, and sensational syncopation.

He pulled out a fresh sheet of paper, stared at his staff,
and let out a high-pitched scream.

Natural yawned. "She was here last night, but she was acting very *unnatural*."

"I agree. She was flat," said Sharp. "Flatter than flat."

"I think her tone was sharp," said Flat. "A little *too* sharp if you ask me."

"ENOUGH! STOP ARGUING!" cried Composer.
"Half Note is missing, and we've got to find her! *Prestissimo!* Fast!"

They searched above the treble clef,
below the bass clef,
and in between every measure.

No Half Note.

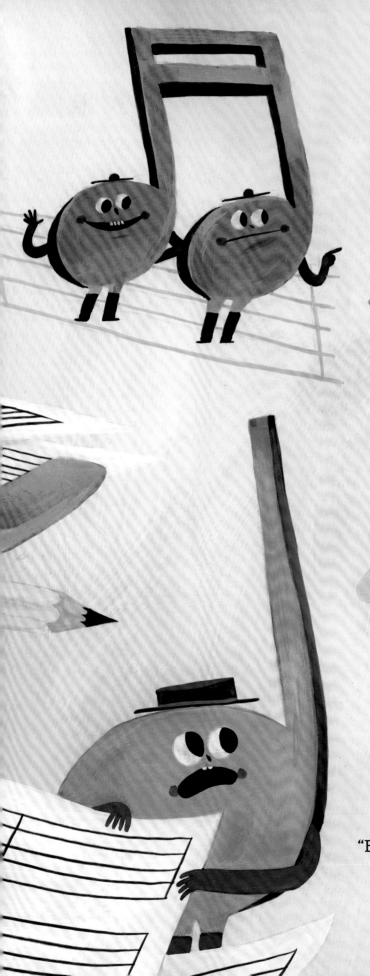

Just then, two Sixteenth Notes strolled by
on their way to rehearsal.

"What are you doing?" they asked.

"We're searching for Half Note," said Whole Note.
"Have you seen her?"

"We passed her on the bridge," they said.
"She was going solo with a strange sack."

"OH NO!" shouted Quarter Note.
"She must be headed to the coda!"

"But the coda is the end of the line!" screeched
the other notes. "We've got to stop her!"

Composer rifled through his stacks of sheet music.
"We'll never find her in time."

"You're right," said Quarter Note. "But maybe there's another way
to bring her back. What if we play her favorite song?"

"Impossible!" said Whole Note. "It's full of half notes."

Composer's eyes lit up.

"What a brilliant idea! Line up everyone! I'm going to need each of you to fill in where Half Note should be. Ready?"

"Ready," said Eighth Note. "But I have a feeling we're going to sound pretty bad."

Quarter Note smiled. "Exactly!"

Half Note had heard Composer's cries and knew the other notes were searching for her, but she tuned them out.

"They don't *really* need me," she sighed. "Two quarter notes can perform my part without a problem, right?"

Her heart pounded *forte*—like a bass drum.

"Well, this is it. I don't know what's waiting for me at the end of the line, but—"

Suddenly, a familiar tune struck a chord with her.

"It's my favorite song! 'Twinkle, Twinkle, Little Star'!"

Only it sounded **OFFBEAT!**

AWFUL!

Downright **DISSONANT!**

"WAIT!" piped up Half Note.
"That's *my* part—not Whole Note's.

"HEY! Why are Quarter Note and Eighth Note
playing there? *I* belong in those spots!

"They are ruining my favorite song.
Somebody has to put a stop to this."

Half Note hurried back as fast
as she could, *accelerando.*

"What kind of arrangement was that?
Composer, how could you let them sound so cacophonous!?"

Composer shrugged. "What else could I do when I'm missing
one of the stars of the musical staff?"

"Me?" Half Note puffed up proudly, feeling noteworthy at last. "I'm done singing the blues."

Jazzed to make music with her friends again, she swung into place.

As the music swelled to a crescendo, Composer applauded. *"Bravissimo!"*

Whole Note agreed. "We don't sound half bad."

Half Note never did feel whole.

But she didn't mind.

She was an instrumental part of the musical staff—and
no one could play her part like she could.

GLOSSARY

NOTABLE NOTES

whole note: a note with the value of four beats

whole rest: a rest (silence) with the value of four beats

half note: a note with the value of two beats

quarter note: a note with the value of one beat

eighth note: a note with the value of a half beat

sixteenth note: a note with the value of a quarter beat

PIECES OF A PIECE

arrangement: a musical piece rewritten with different instruments or voices than the original

bridge: a section of a song that sounds noticeably different from the rest, connecting one part to the next

coda: a section in some musical pieces that brings the song to an end

measure: a small section of the music staff that usually holds four beats

riff: a short section of music that repeats

staff: a set of five horizontal lines and four spaces that each represent a different musical pitch

LOUD AND PROUD

crescendo: a gradual increase in the loudness of a piece of music

forte: loud

PERFECT PITCH

bass clef: marks the bottom lines and spaces of the music staff, where the lower notes are written

chord: a group of two or more notes, usually three, played together

clef: a symbol placed at the beginning of the staff to tell which notes are shown by the lines and spaces

dissonant: sounds wrong, usually when different note pitches don't go well together

flat: a symbol that lowers a note's pitch by a half step

natural: a symbol used to cancel a flat or sharp from a previous note

pitch: how high or low a note sounds

sharp: a symbol that raises a note's pitch by a half step

treble clef: marks the top lines and spaces of the music staff, where the higher notes are written

KEEPING TIME

accelerando: gradually getting faster (accelerating)

beat: a basic unit of time in music

prestissimo: very quick; as fast as possible

syncopation: creating unexpected or offbeat rhythms by stressing certain beats in a piece of music

tempo: the pace of the music, or how fast or slow it is played

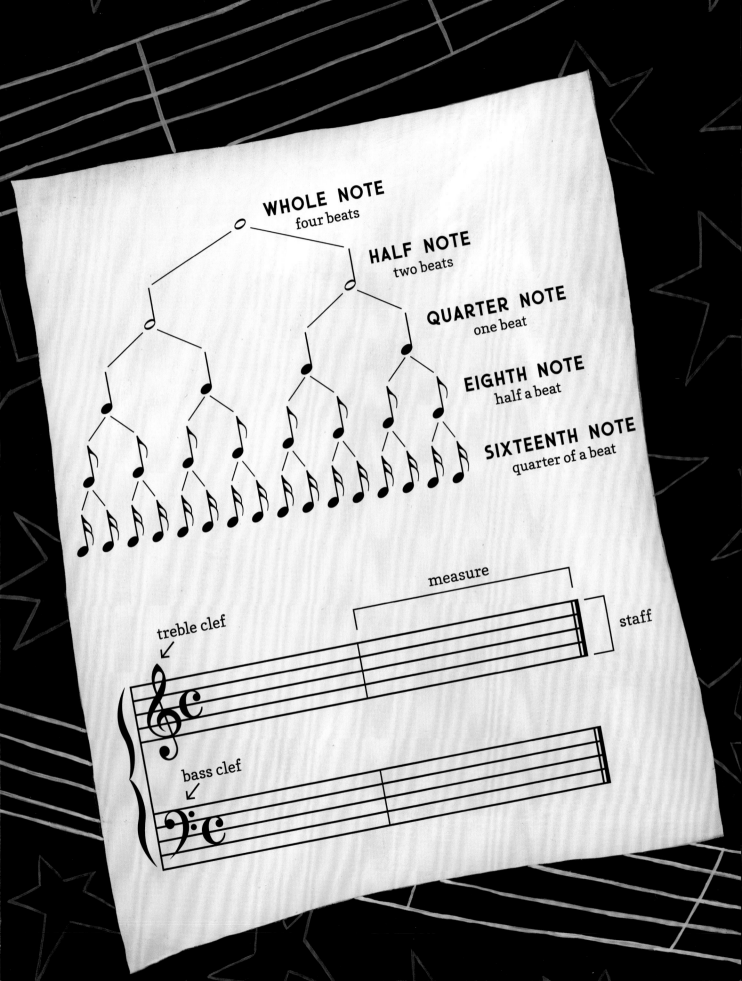